SUCH IS LIFt

MARY ALLISON

For my family, friends and all the hospital staff. Without all of you, I do not think I could have been strong enough to deal with the cancer or the treatment.

Also, for Wessex Cancer Trust and MacMillan Cancer.

Copyright@May 2020 – Mary Allison Version 2 - February 2021

ISBN 979-8648535855

This publication may not be reproduced, stored for retrieval purposes, or copied in any form e.g.: electronic, mechanical, photocopied, recorded etc without written permission of the publisher. Whilst this book is based on true facts about the author under a pseudonym, no names of any people are mentioned. The book has been written to help the author come to terms with a cancer diagnosis and to help people come to terms with their own journey. It is a detailed account of a survivor's story written with honesty and wit.

Chapter One – Again

Oh dear, I thought as I found a lump about a week before our family holiday to Cyprus. Do I stay, do I go? How do I tell my husband, how do I tell our son?

I am convinced it is the "C" word this time. I do not know for sure, but they say a woman knows her own body. After finally plucking up the courage to tell my husband, he checks and agrees that the right side is not the same as the left.

We take a moment, then we discuss the holiday, do I go, do we go? We decide first to call Breast Services at our local hospital. On yes, I forgot to tell you we have been here before. I found a pea sized lump just under a year ago in the same breast. Originally, I was told inconclusive after the mammogram, ultrasound, and biopsy. By the time I got to the operation, I was told not to worry, and everything was fine; relief!! Panic over, so I had the lymph node (plus one found during the operation) removed. Just needed to have an extended Christmas break to recover.

Anyway, back to now, I made the phone call and as I expected it is a new case and I need a doctor's referral.

Dilemma! I asked how long it would be from referral to being I was off on holiday in a week. The answer came back that it might not be long, and I could get an appointment while I am away. We decide to speak to our GP before the holiday. The GP examines me, and we wonder whether it may be hormonal and decide that a week will not make a huge difference. We set up a telephone consultation for our return from holiday.

Off we go on holiday, and funnily enough I do not think about it much as we have a really good time. On the first working day back from holiday after a delay getting home and a diversion to London Heathrow and then a coach back to Gatwick to get the car, I have that chat with the GP.

It is still there, so GP sends off the referral, now the wait. But not for long, I get a date the next day. I have an appointment for another mammogram, ultrasound, and biopsy.

Chapter Two – Diagnosis

I arrived at the hospital in plenty of time, parked and self-checked in at the entrance and got my ticket to show the jumble of letters/numbers. This ticket would be my turn.

I arrived in the Breast Services Outpatients and confirmed I had checked in at the Reception desk. I took a seat and waited after putting another number in the blue tray.

My name was called and for the second time in less than a year my boob was about to be squashed in a press. Oh, my goodness this time it really hurt, probably due to the ping pong ball size lump sitting just above my right nipple. Apparently, I was very brave as I tried not to move an inch. That done I took my seat again to await the next stage, which would highly likely be an ultrasound followed by a biopsy.

Did not have to wait long. The ultrasound confirmed that shown on the mammogram, a much bigger lump than last time. Although I was not told this at the time. I knew another biopsy was about to happen. After about 4 local anaesthetics in various areas of my poor breast, I was reminded I would hear a sound like a staple gun. After a demonstration of the sound, the countdown started to prepare me 3, 2, 1 and I still jumped. Every time in fact right up to the fourth one.

Now I had to get dressed again and make my way back to the reception waiting area to be called in again or told to go. I knew it would be the former. As they say we women know our bodies. I am a realist not a pessimist, I know, trust me! It seemed like the longest wait ever! Eventually I was called in by name rather than the ticket with the numbers and letters.

Then I heard it, confirmation subject to official results of the biopsy that "C" word, CANCER. Oh no surely not me, this happens to other people and other families. I phased out for a while, like I was outside the box looking in at someone else or a fly on the wall. My family hit again for the third time, why?

I managed to gain some sort of focus and the consultant was talking through the process. All I heard were odd words:

- Chemotherapy
- Surgery
- Radiotherapy
- Mastectomy

Not necessarily in that order, but they were words I never thought I would hear. It was going to be a long year! Where do you work? In an NHS environment I replied. No work then, too much risk of infection. Treatment will be for at least six months, loads more tests to follow:

- ECG
- MRI
- CT's
- Regular blood tests
- Oncology

My head was in a spin, emotional and mental overload. It was my sister's wedding anniversary today, so not the best day to receive the news. I would tell mum, but maybe not my sister today. But first I would have to tell my husband. While I was thinking all this, I realised that the Specialist Care Nurse had come in and we are talking more. Scenarios are discussed if CT shows anything else!

I was moved to a comfier consulting room with a sofa. Felt like the relative's room from an Emergency Department like the ones you see on BBC 1's Casualty. It was nice to talk; it was like a mini counselling session. Any questions, how do I feel etc, leaflets, books and how to tell children. Oh, my goodness I had not even though how to tell my nearly 8-year-old son! After a while of chatting, I left and went back to the car, paid the extortionate fee, and drove home. Once home, I sat in the car on our drive. For a moment I smiled as we have only been living here a few months and I thought we have our own drive and parking. I re-focused my thoughts and went indoors.

Shoes and coat off and straight to the lounge to get the phone to call my husband. Think all I said was come please we need to talk. That fifteen-minute journey home for my husband again seemed longer. I cannot remember how I said it, but I know I was brave enough to say the word Cancer. Not sure if I cried, do not think I did? I have not yet, am I normal? There may have been a few tears in my eyes, but I could not cry if I needed to, I am still in shock!!

Chapter 3 – Coming to Terms

Next stage is to wait for results in a week and half, another lifetime.

As I mentioned today is my sister's wedding anniversary, so I will not be telling her and my brother-in-law yet. Do I call mum? I am beginning to hate dilemmas and making decisions already. I told her last time that I had found a lump and we had all the waiting for results. This time I had not told them anything to avoid the worry. Anyway, we decide I do phone them. Hubby gives me some space, cannot remember where he goes, ah yes to collect our son from the childminder and on to the shop after. My brain is already mush. I phone and naturally my mum is shocked especially so soon after the last scare. I am honest and tell her that they are certain, but hope they are wrong.

Then the next day I go into work and tell them, my immediate manager is on holiday so will not know yet. I try to get on with everything and keep busy. No real emotions yet, odd few tears telling some of the girls in the Admin Office.

Time is going slowly today………

Chapter 4 – Results Day

Luckily, it is Thursday today, and I do not have to work. Hubby who has been wonderful so far despite still having to go to his late mum's house every day to sort that out for sale at the end of the month. Did I omit to mention we had another worry/stress going on there? Hey ho, c'est la vie, the house will be gone in a week.

Sorry digressed there, back to the matter in hand. My husband finishes half day on a Thursday, so that is handy too, it means he can come with me and not take any time off work. Our childminder will have our son after school.

We get there and it is confirmed, we finally get to hear what I already knew in my heart, but it is still a shock that nothing or no-one can ever prepare you for. They explain treatment and the suggested medical opinion is chemotherapy, then conservation surgery, followed by radiotherapy. As is routine, they talk about all scenarios just in case they need to follow different paths, e.g., mastectomy.

As a bigger busted woman, I find myself joking a bit about how appealing breast reduction sounds or reconstruction to a smaller size. They either pretended to humour me or they thought I was mad. Then again, I have already established that you need to keep a sense of humour and I convince myself that I am sure they understand and have heard it before.

We then meet with the Speciality Nurse again, albeit a different one this time. Back on that comfy sofa, I finally break down in my husband's arms. I am so glad he is there, and I notice he has a few tears too. We have a chat with the nurse after composing myself and we go and get our son as if nothing happened. At home I am still composed, even after confirming results to family and how things will happen. Yesterday was our son's 8th birthday so have not told him yet. I will always remember September 2016.

Chapter 5 – Scans and Tests

After results day, today is ECG blood test and trying to arrange for removal of Mirena coil.

ECG and blood tests all get done by 11am, so I decide to go doctors to sort the coil. No!! They are closing during the morning/early afternoon until 2pm for training. I know they need to do it, but it has rattled me it has to be today. After a major rant to myself and other disgruntled patients who may or may not be listening, I try one of the other surgeries, but they are all closed for training. I go home angry and disappointed. I phone them later and arrange for one morning next week.

Back to work today Monday and my manager is also back from holiday. She has heard the news now and says she is so sorry to hear. I update her on my progress so far. Even though colleagues are finding out slowly, today is not too bad and everyone is incredibly supportive.

Today is fire alarm test day for the annual drill. I get my son to the childminder at 7.45am so I can get to work at 8.15am. I do not believe the traffic delays. I am on adrenaline by the time I get there, and the fire drill goes well. But I am mentally drained and struggled through the day.

Wednesday, coil removed this morning and nurse says about precautions. Think I know by now, but guess they have to say it. Sex is the last thing on my mind. We are not planning any more children luckily anyway. Back at work after doctors and it is not a good day. I have not managed to do a lot of the work I had hoped to do and expected to do. I have been left disappointed with myself. I broke down in tears and explained to my manager that I am emotionally and mentally exhausted. We got together and put a plan into place. It was agreed I would tidy up the smaller jobs to pave the way for my manager to take over. Being off work for a long time makes me feel guilty which I know is silly, but I hope they manage OK without me. I will be deciding soon when I am finishing.

Back to tests – I now know when my CT scans are. Appointments are also arranged for Oncologist and for MRI scan. It seems that I am nearly ready to go with treatment.

I now have a nice weekend to look forward to – a mini break!

Chapter 6 - Weekend Break at Mum & Dad'

Saturday morning, looking forward to today as I drive to Mum and Dad's for a mini break.

Be good I say to my boys as I leave to drive in the rain – typical!! Mind you the weather is better now than an hour ago as we woke to thunder and lightning.

I finally arrived at my parents after a horrid wet slow journey.

Dad made me jump out of my skin as I was not expecting him to be home. I did wonder why the house alarm did not cheap at me to deactivate it. They had been to the doctors to get their flu jabs and obviously did not have to wait long.

We had a cup of coffee, my first of the day (I cannot drink coffee before a long drive – weak bladder!), while we decide where to go for lunch. Unfortunately, bar tickets for the lounge at football are extremely hard to come by shame.

We decide on a pub and then on our way we see the traffic jam on the main road going the other way. We hope the pub is not too busy otherwise we might be late for football and my parents' space in the car park will be gone if the traffic is still there on the way back. We enjoy a nice lunch, as usual paid for by my mum and dad! I have a half of bitter shandy as I am such a lightweight now. The meal and service as always is excellent at this pub.

We take the risk in the traffic and luckily get to the game in good time. I buy my ticket, correction my mum does, and they are so kind.

We meet my dad in the club shop as there is a jacket he wants to buy. Mum asks if I want one too. So, we order two. The jacket is special as it has the family name on as a shareholder. I say to mum that I will add it to the cheque with the presents for my nephew's birthday.

The game itself is very mediocre, both sides play awfully bad long ball football. Not our style at all. As usual the ref is naff, and everyone complains. Then suddenly we wake up due to some substitutions which should have been made an hour before and we score. This win moves us up from near relegation to mid table, but it is all awfully close in the division this year. Once we get home we settle on the sofa and after a while have tea and cake before watching Strictly Come Dancing on BBC1. This is one thing I really love, sitting down with Mum and Dad (before he goes to the study) watching Strictly Come Dancing and Casualty on a Saturday night. Reminds me of my younger days. Soon it is time for bed for me, it is 10'oclock.

Sunday morning, after breakfast Mum and I go to church. This is the church where I grew up, got baptised, confirmed, and married the first time. I used to sing in the choir when I was little too. The service was good, but I could not sing one song as it triggered too much emotion and the words were hard to sing. But I just about managed to hold it together. We stayed for coffee and I caught up with a particularly good friend of mine, who I also played badminton with many years ago. She was terribly upset to hear I had cancer. Mum found it extremely hard to listen to me talking and was comforted by my friend's mother who was also there. After a nice catch up about the nicer things in life too, we went home for a nice roast lunch with Dad. After an all too short visit and some big hugs goodbye, I made my way home in lovely sunshine to see my boys at home.

Chapter 7 – More Scans etc

Monday is CT scan day, and I am terrified. I had an MRI a few years ago before my shoulder surgery and it was horrid. My fears were warranted after the iodine was put in the warm glow was a bit unpleasant, then the feeling of needing the loos; but then I started to shake as if I was terrified. I could not wait to get out of there. It stopped briefly after the chest and pelvis part of the scan. Now the head scan, which was even worse, but I managed to get through it. Still shaking a bit, I walked back home.

Tuesday – back to work this morning and it goes reasonably well. I finish early today and meet my husband back at home as we go to see the Oncologist to discuss chemotherapy. We must wait a while and as always it is torture. I am hoping she will be able to give me some idea of the CT results. Subject to the radiologist agreeing we hear the word "curable". For the first time since diagnosis, I feel some weight lift off me.

I am given a blood test form, details of a wig company who will contact me and we hope to start treatment in a couple of weeks. We talked about the "cold cap" which stops hair loss. But I am advised that as my hair is already so fine, it is best to let it fall out as the cold cap makes your hair finer. Apparently, I also must have a clip insert to help monitor the reduction of the lump. It will also act as a marker if the lump were to completely disappear.

Today is Wednesday and I am at work this morning unexpectedly as the Oncologist said I could work as back staff in the surgery. Another not bad day at work. My colleagues were surprised but pleased to hear I could work when I felt well enough. My son has football today, so hubby is on standby to get him in case I am shaking too much after the MRI later. I get there and go straight in after taking an age to park. Why are my appointments always at the busiest time! In I go, I must lie on the bed face down and my boobs must go in a special part of the equipment with a space for my head. This is comfy but a bit weird. I am given some headphones and a panic button I prepare mentally for this "treat" for at least half an hour. It seems much easier being face down and I manage to zone out. I cannot hear the music well due to the drill noises and loud bangs of the scanner, but amazingly I almost fall asleep several times. All done after a long time, but I survived, so well in fact that I call hubby and say I can pick up our little monkey from football. He is disappointed as he was hoping to finish work early. Tomorrow is Thursday and my last Thursday off work as I have agreed I will take Tuesday off going forward so I can regularly attend a support group where my friend is a volunteer befriender.

Chapter 8 – Day off and normality

Took my son to school and followed up with breakfast at Costa and some retail therapy. I bought myself some new boots as my feet were getting wet in my old ones and a new black skirt for work. I also bought my parents a board game called Logo for Christmas. I do not think I have ever bought a Christmas present in October. First time for everything, I guess!

Now back home relaxing, writing this, after a bit of housework and starting to feel sleepy.

Today is Friday and my long day at work. It is usual accounts day, tied in with end of year journal. Aagghh! I input the journal and the balance is out, so I leave a message for the accountants to call me next week as something is not quite right. I do not want to do the minor adjustment journals until this is correct. Time flies by and it is not if I expected it to be, probably because I am so busy.

Saturday – hooray! Lie in today; and we managed to encourage our little man to go back to bed for a bit longer. Daddy got up and I had even longer. We all then had breakfast and went to the swimming pool in town for our son's lesson. On the way home we went to the scout hut to get his Cub uniform. Oh, how time flies and how grown up he is getting suddenly. After lunch at home the boys went out to Bognor Regis and I had a lazy afternoon. They got home just as I was prepping dinner. A letter from Oncology arrived today to disrupt the normality saying chemo starts next Friday, slightly earlier than I envisaged. Good news, but somehow, I am feeling a bit mentally drained suddenly.

But still a bit of normality to go as today is Sunday and it is Church choir singing day.

Chapter 9 – Chemotherapy 1

Monday was pretty much a normal workday. Fire alarm test which has not been done for a couple of weeks – oops! And trying to tie up that pesky journal.

Tuesday – Day off as changing from Thursdays now you may remember. My first morning at the local Cancer Support group and a chance to catch up with my bestie who volunteers there. It was great and I stayed all morning, meeting some great and very brave people, who inspired me.

Wednesday – Oncology pre chemotherapy appointment today, which I have to say, went well. I found it hard signing the consent form hearing written words such as "death" even though it is curable. CT scan was given as all OK today. Lots of blood tests and PICC line flushes to book and I came out feeling overwhelmed. Hubby dropped me off back home and the reality of it all hit me; I had a silly melt down moment, saying I could not go through with it all. Then I saw the look on his face, the tears in his eyes and I apologised immediately for my selfish behaviour. We got into our respective cars and went to work, although I only got as far as the roundabout at the bottom of the hill and turned around to go back home. I called work to say my head was spinning, then my husband too and then promptly went to bed and slept for the rest of the afternoon.

Thursday – PICC line and clip in today at the hospital. First one I am dreading as it is a permanent cannula to make it easy to send the treatment straight towards the veins. Also used for blood tests and must be flushed out weekly/during treatment. It was put in using ultrasound and a special magnetic board on the chest which talks to a magnet on the end of the PICC line. Now me being awkward, having had lymph node surgery just under a year ago, means that the line must go in my left arm. This is fine, but it means I must wait longer as the line has to go the long way round to get into the right place, near the heart. To put the line in, I have a local anaesthetic called Lidocaine. I have heard about this at work at the surgery and find it is certainly numbing your arm like a dead weight. There was no way I was going to feel anything or move it. But I was not prepared for the numbness and tingling when I went to move it. Once in I had the x-ray to check the placement which was all fine. After 2 hours, I quickly popped back home for lunch before my 3.15 appointment for the clip. After an hour's wait and an injection, it was a small surgical procedure not dissimilar to a biopsy. It was all done and steri-stripped very quickly – piece of cake. Our son was picked up by his Dad from after school club today, so I called them to come and collect me.

Friday – Chemo day today – its arrived, I am up at 6.45 and dress by 7.00. I need to ensure I have a good breakfast today I decide, and I have been drinking plenty of water/squash. I say bye to the boys (hubby helping today with school) and head off for work for 7.45 – 11.45 today, as chemo is this afternoon. All goes well and quickly luckily. Sad news though, my colleague's mum has lost her battle against a long illness and she is not in. I will send my thoughts to her a bit later today. I am ready to go, but a query comes up just as I am about to leave – typical. I get away just before 12 noon. I heat up some Chinese for lunch and I am about to tuck in when both my boys walk through the door. My husband had to pick up our son from school, following a call to say that the swollen testicle he had a while ago has flared up. He is due a follow up for probably surgery sometime soon, but we decide to call Urology to see if we can go in. As I am due to meet my friend at about 1pm for coffee before my chemo (she is coming with me for the first one), I transfer my lunch into a plastic container and eat in the car on the way down to the hospital. Boys wait a call back from Urology, while I go off for my medicine. My phone is about run out of charge, so I hope I can charge it while I am there, my friend seems to think I can.

We enjoy a chat about chemo and how rubbish things can be in life, as well as a good catch up as we have not seen each other for some time now. We head towards Oncology and do not wait too long before I am shown to a room and the nurse goes through all the formalities of consent and side effects. I am first given an anti-sickness tablet while everything is prepared. They flush the PICC line to sterilise it and check there are no blockages. I am on a treatment called FECT, the first course of 3 are the FEC and the second course of 3 are the T. They all stand for something, but I cannot remember, but Google if you are interested.

After a while we start with a red solution, the first of three each time as part of the FEC treatment. This red solution is pumped in very slowly by the nurse into my PICC line. The first dose of this was the largest and is followed by two smaller ones. The PICC line is flushed again and is following by the other two medicines which are pumped through automatically with a flush in between and after. After about 4 hours, I am all done and given a concoction of drugs to taken home, steroids, anti-sickness, and injections to do at home (help). It is all communicated well and written down on the packets when to do what and how many.

After no reception on my phone, luckily, I had been able to charge it, I find out my son is OK, and that Urology will see him in a few weeks as planned. I felt a little rough at odd moments throughout the treatment including a metallic taste in my mouth and a sore throat at times, but I am ok now, so enjoy a nice small meal at home. I have an early night after bedtime story for my son and a bit of TV with my husband. Just before bed I take a steroid tablet, as the chemo was in the afternoon, going forward I will take one first thing in the morning and the second after lunch.

Chapter 10 – Chemo Recovery

Slept OK last night; did not think I would. I had a bowl next to my bed just in case. Should have taken the steroid slightly earlier as it took me a while to get to sleep! And I do not feel sick – amazingly happy about that. Just have a bit of a headache today but drinking lots of fluids. Bought some constipation tablets (not needed yet) and ordered my waterproof picc-line sleeve for baths and showers.

It is Saturday today, had a catch up on the phone with my sister while my husband took our son for his swimming lesson. They came home for a snack lunch and I have taken my tablets as required and will continue throughout the day. Some housework this afternoon, but mostly been relaxing with Twilight and The Lion, The Witch, and the Wardrobe while the boys are visiting IKEA and Toys R Us. Our son is spending his birthday vouchers in Toys R Us today. I am looking forward to Strictly Come Dancing, Casualty and reading in bed later before seeing what Sunday and the rest of the week brings.

Aah injections time! I cannot do it; I have a dreadful fear of needles. I call my doctors surgery, but they are not able to fit me in for just 5 minutes. Not impressed, double aah!! I call Acute Oncology and explain. They do it for me the first couple of times, then the third time I do it myself, so I can do the last two at home. Well done me, so proud of myself. Ready for next time.

Chapter 11 – A bit of Normality

I have not put pen to paper for a while. I have had some normality lately with two days back at work. Felt very tired but it was nice to see everyone and occupy the mind.

I enjoyed the October half term holidays with my son. We had a DVD day, went to the cinema to watch The Trolls, followed by lunch at Frankie & Benny's. My sister came down to see us one day and we went to Gunwharf Quays and took a trip up the Spinnaker Tower. My son was lying on the glass face down, but for my sister and me it was enough of a challenge just to walk on it, but we managed it.

As Daddy is not working Fridays, they went to Bovingdon Tank Museum for the day and I went back to work.

Friday is invoicing and Accounts day, but it was even busier as I had lots to catch up on.

Chapter 12 – A stinking cold

Well, I ended my lovely half term week by coming down with a sore throat followed by a stinking cold. Not been at work at all this week. It got to Wednesday, I felt so awful I phoned Acute Oncology and they suggested getting antibiotics from my GP. After a couple of days taking the tablets, come Friday it is slowly clearing up.

Feeling rubbish, prompted me to make a tough but sensible decision, no more work until treatment is complete. At least my employers now know where they are and will not be worrying about whether I am coming in today, tomorrow, or next week. I too will have less stress and can be part of important groups and therapies.

Chapter 13 – Round 2

As I knew what to expect, this time did not seem as bad as round 1. However, there was some self-inflicted sickness as I messed up my steroids by only taking one tablet twice a day instead of two. But easily remedied, I took one of my emergency anti sickness and the steroids on an extra day. Good week was a good week, no colds infecting me.

I feel like getting up and about a bit more this time, which I am sure, is making me feel better.

Chapter 14 – Little Sis' birthday

We went to see family at the end of my good week, to celebrate my sister's birthday and early celebration for my husband's birthday a week later. It was lovely to see everyone for a change as there was no swimming gala for my niece, so all were there at the family meal.

On the Saturday prior I went to watch my team play football, hoping I would not jinx them and ruin their good run. I had lunch in the ground bar with my parents and their footie friends. Luckily, their winning streak continued. My boys went up to London for the day we met them back at home later for a cup of tea and a slice of cake.

Chapter 15 – Round 3

And off we go again, pre chemo blood test and oncology today. Oncology reports are incredibly positive, as the lump is much softer and harder to find.

Found round 3 hard. As I write this, I am feeling extremely sick and tired. Had the steroid intravenously today for some reason which I was warned would make me feel worse. This was a complete understatement, but I am remaining positive. I will be taking an anti-sickness tablet in a moment so that should help.

I have a fantastic friend who took my son to school again today after driving me to my 8.30 chemo. She is a star as she also picked him up from school so I can rest today. Here is hoping I feel better after an early night!

I can spend the next couple of weeks carrying on with Christmas shopping.

Chapter 16 – Finishing Christmas Shopping

Think I have finished and got the last presents now. I bought some wine, chocolates and a Christmas cactus for my mum's lovely friend and her husband, as a thank you for supporting my parents during my treatment. My mum's friend was a lollipop lady for my sister and me when we were at primary school. It has really comforted me to know that being miles away from my family there is someone there to take them out and keep them company.

Just about everything wrapped now, just husbands to do and I need to talk to "Santa!"

Chapter 17 – Aching

Oh, my goodness do I ache, my legs and feet. I have early stages of osteo-arthritis in both hips which is made worse with this horrible medication in my system. And from what I have heard the next stage will make it worse – joy!

I am taking paracetamol as required to take the edge off the pain, but it does not really make a huge amount of difference.

Chapter 18 – The weekend before Christmas

And at the end of a good week, I am OK except the muscles. We are off to Nottingham this Saturday to see Andre Rieu's Christmas Concert. After a 5½ hour journey in horrid fog with lots of accidents we arrive. We check into our hotel and get to the room. My husband is tired as he drove all the way.

Just as he lies on the bed, he gets a text to say the show is cancelled. One of his orchestra members has had a heart attack and is in a critical condition in hospital. We stay anyway and drive back next day. We had a lovely meal in the hotel that evening. There was a group of people at the hotel who were also meant to be going to the concert.

Journey back is only 3½ hours which is much better, partly because we avoid the M25 this time just in case.

After a couple of hours at home, it is 9 Lessons and Carols at church. I am singing in the choir once again and am doing a reading. I am really looking forward to this service as it must be 30 years since I have sung in the choir at it. It will be my last service at church for sure now as I need to start taking it easier as the chemo changes next week and I am getting more tired.

Chapter 19 – All change

Today I had the change of chemotherapy. A friend from church came along for some reassurance.

The chemo was shorter only an hour and a half. There were no immediate side effects like metallic tastes in my mouth during treatment.

I feel OK after the treatment and get ready to think about a family Christmas at my sister's.

Chapter 20 – My little man

My little man had a small operation yesterday too, so all go!

My wonderful husband took charge at hospital, just in case because I am going to have chemo tomorrow.

The whole experience made me very emotional as our son was so brave. I think had our brave 8-year-old been sad, I would have been braver.

Still, we both have an excuse to cuddle up on the sofa and watch DVDs together.

Chapter 21 – Christmas

It is Christmas Eve today, I am feeling very tired after my 4th chemo, but ok to travel to family thankfully! We are all packed ready to go and we decide we will travel after a snack lunch at home. Our son has recovered well and will be able to enjoy a nice bath for the first time since his operation when we are at Granny and Grandpa's house.

We arrive and I particularly am so happy to be there. Mum has cooked a meal for us as always on our arrival.

Today is Christmas Day and the little man sleeps in until 8 o'clock after waking up at 5 o'clock rather excited. He came to our room saying is it Christmas yet? We said no and he went back to bed. But come 8 o'clock we could hold off his excitement no more as Father Christmas had been and we must wake quickly to see him open his presents. Lots of chocolates, bath toys etc and then suddenly the excitement of the magic set he had asked Father Christmas for. What a lucky little boy and we have already learnt how to do two tricks ready to show Granny and Grandpa at breakfast time. I can see this is going to be painful!!

To save time at my sister's house before lunch we, that is me, husband, and son, open our presents to each other. My husband has been thoughtful; he has bought me some lip balm as my lips get very dry with my treatment and some dark nail varnish to hide my horrid yellow nails. He always buys me some nice Wilkinson bath and showers gels/creams. My son helped choose a lot of presents. I have a brilliant pair of boys.

We go to my sister's house and to my bro-in-law's wonderful cooking. As the kids (our son, my niece and nephew) are excited we do not waste too much time and we get opening some wonderful presents. I also have a great family.

We enjoy a pre-lunch drink; even I have a gin and tonic as I am feeling amazingly good today. I am probably running on the adrenaline and excitement.

Soon it is time for Christmas lunch. Yum, Turkey, roast pots, lots of vegetables and cauliflower cheese which my husband hates! I fill my plate and amazingly I eat the lot and I also polish off some Christmas pudding AND Black Forest Gateau. I hear you say Gateau for Christmas, but it is essential for my brother-in-law as it is my mum's speciality and his favourite. Luckily, we are allowed some too.

I have a couple of glasses of red wine, but my taste buds do not really enjoy them, so I enjoy a couple of gin and tonics during the latter part of the day. We enjoy some games, and we all collapse to bed by 11pm. A wonderful Christmas Day, the only downside I could not enjoy all the soft cheeses.

Chapter 22 – Boxing Day and Catching up

Halfway through my course of 7 injections this time for my blood cells pick up. I awake today and my legs ache so badly that by the time I get down for breakfast I am in tears. I take some paracetamol which helps a bit as I left my co-codamol at home.

Mid-morning, we say goodbye to my sister and family before going back to my parents for a few days.

I do start to feel a bit better throughout the day. The rest of the day is nice and restful.

Well, that was Christmas, and it is time to go home tomorrow. Today we are catching up with my mum's friend and her husband. We have not seen them at Christmas for a while. I give them their gifts as a thank you for being there for my parents during all our treatments and illnesses especially me as we do not live locally. We have some lovely chats, and our son shows them some magic tricks.

It seems ages ago that this friend was the lollipop lady for my sister and I when we were at infant and junior schools. Which means we have known them as a family for about 40 or so years. How time flies.

Chapter 23 – New Year

This feels exceedingly difficult; I do not want to celebrate. Our son has been hard work again since we got home from family and tensions are high. I want to share champagne during the evening, but I find my husband has gone to bed! With my menopausal side effects, I flip, and arguments start, and he gets his coat to go out. I apologise in floods of tears and drag him back in the house. We talk and eventually things are better. We enjoy a drink and decide to save the rest of the champers for when I am feeling better and more like celebrating something. Just after midnight we go to bed and have a big hug. In a way it was good as we got rid of a lot of tension. We love each other so much and have a wonderful friendship which has kept us going through lots of tough times since meeting nearly 15 years ago.

Chapter 24 – January

So, I have had 5 treatments of 6 now, nearly there! I received some flowers today from mum and dad to say nearly there.

The hot flushes are become more frequent now with the menopause. The aching legs are worse too and I am totally exhausted, but apart from that I continue to do well. I am resting a lot more now. In fact, today as I watched the Australian Open Tennis, I fell asleep which is something I often struggle to do during the day.

I cannot believe we are almost halfway through January already, but I am so glad as my final chemotherapy will be in a week and a half's time. Back soon with the next update.

Chapter 25 – Final Chemo Cycle

Home from the last chemotherapy and I am so tired. Just so glad now they are all done. Hopefully, I will have a bit of time to recover before surgery date.

Day 3 of the cycle and last lot of injections commence today, and I really start to feel the fatigue and the stress of the injections. I will be glad when they are all over.

Day 7 of the cycle, my bones ache so much, and the emotions are so high. What a hurdle this chemo was, but I have wonderful family and friends who have helped me through, plus my support group at the local cancer centre. My counsellor is brilliant, and she helps me keep positive.

Everyone said all the way through how well I look, and I have to say I have been incredibly lucky with illnesses. Having said that I am today coming down with my son's cold. I woke up this morning feeling so full of it. I have never felt so rough. My friend has texted me after school today and offered to take my son to school tomorrow. Bless her she is wonderful; it means I can have a PJ day as it is Friday, my husband does the afterschool run.

Feel a bit better now I am resting, knowing it is the weekend. I have a pre op date already, which is good I guess, so this is not too much of a gap after the end of chemo.

Chapter 26 – Prep for Surgery

Pre op day and my obs are a bit low, but they seem happy, so fingers crossed. I get home and begin to feel rubbish again. I do not need a full blown cold now, or the earache to go with it!

I have less than a week to get over this cold, but I am getting worse. It is so bad I am having to take Lemsip which I find repulsive. I take the blackcurrant one as it is mildly better than the lemon one. But it works and by today I am starting to feel loads better.

I have a cooling gel pad which fits inside my pillow. It is amazing and helps manage the hot much better and wake up feeling quite a bit more refreshed.

My bag is packed, and I have new button up PJs and tops for ease of dressing post op. Two sleeps before a 6.30am pick up by taxi.

Chapter 27 – The Op!

Well, here it is, the day has arrived. Not ready for this as I am too tired, but it gets another hurdle done.

It is Monday 13th February and tomorrow are Valentine's Day! Sorry husband hardly romantic to pick up the wife from hospital.

I arrive nil by mouth since midnight. Luckily, I am not hungry yet as it is still only just my usual breakfast time. I had a few cups of water at 6am or just before. I discover that I am 4th on the list today, so it could be a long wait and depends on the needs of other patients.

It gets to about 12 noon, I start thinking I am a bit hungry, but I cannot even have some water. I go back to my magazine that I have already read twice. 1pm, bored now and not in the mood for my novel today; feeling sleepy so I put my head back and doze. Suddenly I get woken up by someone being called, sadly not me. It is now 2pm and I am hungry. Taking my mind of things, I get out my novel and surprisingly I get into it a bit more. Before I know it is 3.30pm.

It must be my turn soon; I have been here for hours now and am starving. The afternoon slots have started to go in for their operations and I am still waiting. I have a wander to stretch my legs. Then after a while of pacing and reading, at 4.45 my name is finally called. I get to have a nice sleep now and a snack hopefully when I wake up.

I awake feeling very groggy as I usually do after a general anaesthetic. Then the realisation a drain attached to me, no!

I find out I am waiting on a bed in A Ward. They are busy and do not have much bed space available. It turns out there is no space on A Ward, and I end up on the top floor of the hospital in the private ward. I have a room of my own, a consulting room turned into a room for me as they are so short staffed, nice but lonely.

I remember I was offered something to eat but could not tell you what. I also remember some vague conversation saying it all went well and that I would be here overnight. Then bad news, I would go home with the drain for up to a week, dependent on fluid build-up.

I have a reasonable night's sleep considering except the wakeups for obs and meds. Before I know it, the wakeup call is appreciated – breakfast time and a cup of coffee which is bliss.

After breakfast I am helped to **my** bathroom to have a wash with a bowl of warm water, as I am unable to have a shower while I have the drain fitted, then I am left to do this by myself. It is a bit of a challenge, but I just about make it. I get dressed just in time for my lunch to arrive.

Hopefully, I will be going home soon. The nurse and doctor have their respective chats about care of the drain. I am to have a district nurse coming to measure fluids and drain until I feel confident myself. My husband has been phoned and we await medication from the pharmacy. Eventually I get to go home after a long wait for the pills! Hooray home time – Happy Valentine's Day darling x.

Chapter 28 – Op Recovery

Well sleeping with this drain at home is horrible especially when you must get up two or three times a night. I have a lovely little bag to hold it in and help me to carry it about.

I must lie on my back and cannot move so have to sleep in a very unnatural position for me. My lovely husband is going to do the school run for the next couple of weeks or so as I cannot go out due to the risk of infection.

The district nurse is coming today after my first rubbish sleep at home. When she arrives, she checks the amounts in there, loads – deep joy. She shows me how to check and drain it but will come again tomorrow just in case.

And so, I do not do much today apart from sit and feel sorry for myself watching television. I am an emotional mess worse than I have been throughout the treatment so far. The day passes by so slowly and I have another restless night.

Today is the last day the district nurse will visit, but I must phone them every day to let them know how much fluid is in the drain until it is 40ml or less for two consecutive days. The drain can only come out if this happens, but not before one week and it must be removed by day ten regardless.

She is worried about my emotional state as I keep crying on the phone. As it is half term next week I am so determined to get to my parents for a week with my son. This will also give my husband a well-deserved break. If I cannot go my husband will just drive up my son for the week. I need help to recover a bit while my husband is at work and really do not want to be alone.

They phone every day and I have an appointment in a few days at the Breast Services department on Monday of half term week for a surgery check and HOORAY they agree to take it out. My husband has taken the day off work to look after our son, so we pack once home, and he drives us there. We have a wonderful time and go to a farm to feed animals, bowling, and a meal out. Before we know it is all over and time to go. We meet Daddy halfway to pick us up.

Chapter 29 – Radiotherapy Preparation

No rest for the wicked as they say. No truer words could be spoken as I now prepare for radiotherapy. Before this can happen however, I must attend appointments to check fluid build-up and the first one is today.

It does look like there is still a lot of fluid there. I see my surgeon and he get about 250ml out. Good thing I am numb under my arm from the lymph nodes removal and there was no need for an anaesthetic as I could feel nothing. I will have to return until they are satisfied, they are not getting much out. In total I have another three of these appointments. Finally, I am done, and I can be referred for radiotherapy. So, I play the waiting game once again for my planning appointment.

The day arrives and I have a scan first to check the position of my breast markers which were inserted before surgery to help with the alignment. They lie me down on the bed under a radiotherapy scanner and I have three little dots of tattoo ink injected into various places. Ouch really hurt. Now they must line up with the lasers and get the bed to the right height etc for the actual radiotherapy to begin. This will give them the measurements for each session which I start in a couple of weeks after the school Easter holidays.

Chapter 30 – Radiotherapy Begins

The first one of nineteen sessions arrive or fifteen plus four as they call it. The fifteen being three weeks plus four boosters which are more intensive.

The time goes quickly for my first few as I am in on time. Even when I have a delay it is only about forty-five minutes, usually when a scanner breaks down. The staff have all been brilliant trying to get us on a different machine as quickly as possible.

Before I know it, I am having my halfway review and I am talking with them about side effects after all the line-up is double checked. I explain the main thing is feeling tired, but I am coping better than at the start. I can swim now and drinking more water which has boosted my energy levels. The area concerned is not too red and not at all sore, so the shed load of aqueous cream is doing its job.

I am now on the final four boosters. They position everything differently after more scans to check the repositioning. All done, so now I am into the final three sessions. With three to go, I am sitting here in the waiting room with a thirty-minute wait and I have left my phone at home which is annoying. My husband will be annoyed as he has probably texted me to ask who is picking up our son. I should be able to get home just in time to reply before going straight out again to collect the little man.

Before I know it, I am all done and home having finished all treatments, now I start my remission. Who would have thought, what a journey it has been?

I am feeling tired but overall, good. Then suddenly after a few days I feel very sore under my right boob. I get my husband to have a look and it is all blistered like bad sunburn. I must go bra free for a few days, which is not comfortable when you are a little on the large side! However, it is more comfortable, and I try all manner of aqueous creams etc, discovering that the recommended Vaseline is not the best remedy. After a few weeks it finally starts to heal, and I finally feel like I am in remission.

Chapter 31 – The start of the rest of my life

That strange feeling of trying to get back to a normal life is starting to hit me now. I feel odd and need my counsellor more than ever now as I feel abandoned with no hospital appointments until my mammogram in September, which is four months away.

I chat with my counsellor and say I am thinking of discussing with the doctor about starting anti-depressants as I feel so slow now it is all over. I think the realisation of what I have been through and how it has affected the rest of the family, particularly my son is starting to sink in.

She and the doctor agree this will be a good course of action and I get a prescription for Sertraline as I can only take certain ones due to confliction with the Tamoxifen. By now we are in July and the Tamoxifen is beginning to take its toll slightly affecting the menopausal symptoms more, the hot flushes are more intense at night mixed now with horrid night's sweats. I am told that the Sertraline will help with this which they do seem to a bit.

I still have one or two weeks each month where I notice the menopause more. I am now using lavender remedies such as pillow sprays which really do aid sleep and help relax me.

Before I know it, we are in September and it is a year since the scan for diagnosis. I am today having a mammogram to check all is still good. Again, a wait of two weeks for the results and all good news thanks goodness. I will have an appointment in February with my surgeon once again to check everything is OK with the scar tissue. He will also do a check for anything suspicious as another back up.

I have decided I am not returning to work at the surgery and enjoying being a lady of leisure to think about me and my family. However, I failed to tell you about my little volunteer job I have been doing since July ....

Chapter 32 – Part time Volunteer

I am now Volunteer Treasurer for my local church. I was asked by the Vicar (for whom I had helped with Sunday School teaching for several years pre cancer) if I would like to join the PCC (Parochial Church Council). I agreed but had a feeling that I was going to be asked to help with the accounts. The Vicar had hoped it would not be that obvious, but as he had my CV from a previous job, I applied for it was not difficult to fathom. Anyway, we met for a chat and discussed the options. I could work from home and would meet up at the Vicarage every now and then to do Payroll and go through any queries as required. At the beginning of the next year, it would become a paid role, just a few hours a week as a Bookkeeper.

I feel really chuffed to have been asked and am really enjoying it. It will be a nice little earner next year. I must attend a monthly finance meeting and PCC and DCC meetings every now and then too.

As I joined the choir just before my diagnosis, it is nice to be back singing now since my break during treatment. My son is now also a member and is looking forward to becoming a fully-fledged chorister soon into the new year.

Chapter 33 – A normal Christmas

We finally have a normal Christmas with everyone well and no-one recovering from operation or illnesses.

I can eat all the cheese I want and can finally taste wine as I have already tested this several times.

It is wonderful to have another lovely Christmas with my family with my brother-in-law cooking another fabulous lunch and more lovely Black Forest Gateau made by mum.

On Boxing Day morning, I can say yes to Eggs Benedict, yum.

We meet up with my mum's brother at their house. They downsized a year or so ago and it is the first time we have been there. They hold an open house for all the family with a genuinely nice buffet lunch. We reminisce on the old years when they used to go to Barbados a lot and bring back rum by having a glass of the famous Mount Gay. Again yum!

Before we know it once again it is time to go home but at least this year it is back to our normal routines and it feels like it will be a New Year this time.

Chapter 34 – Normality

I am now working for the church as a paid Bookkeeper 3 hours a week and loving it. Church choir is going well, and my son is now a proper chorister. Saw the surgeon and all is still good.

Did I say normality, my son is struggling to cope, and he has been diagnosed with mild traits of ADHD and Autism Spectrum Condition. As we thought, he shows some signs of mild autism. He has had some Counselling sessions as well which has really helped him to try to manage his anger. He is working hard to kerb his frustrations now. Time to think about the impact it has had on him.

We have booked to return to Cyprus this year after our trip to a lovely hotel last year. We will be at the same place and hopefully will hire a car. Our friends who own a villa will be out at a similar time, so we hope to meet up with them.

I am enjoying being back at my son's school Thursday afternoons listening to reading. He is thriving with his Athletics/Cross Country and is looking forward to the school cup again this year. He took part in a series of local short runs and did very well with his school and alongside other schools in the area. He also plays badminton after school too and looks forward to returning to Tennis having decided Football needs a break.

Chapter 35 – Looking forward

Before I end the book, I would like to thank everyone listed at the front of this book and many more unmentioned who have helped me throughout my treatment and on the way to recovery.

I can hardly believe what has happened to me, but I do not feel bitter as I have been lucky and am able to look forward now and enjoy life to the full. Yes, I do get tired and have bad days. Damp and cold weather plays havoc with my osteo-arthritis which is getting worse all the time. But I am still here so I will take all the problems that come with recovery and the medications I must take.

Maybe one day I will go back to working a bit more, maybe I will not we will have to see what turns my life takes along the way. For the time being I am concentrating on improving every day, taking it all in my stride and enjoying the challenges of every new day to the best of my ability.

As I finish the book, I will in two months' time be a year in remission. I have lost a good friend I had met through a cancer group on the way, but this has taught me a valuable lesson in life; it is what it is, our life is mapped out and we must follow the path. It is all fate, and I will end with three words which I hope you will take away with you into your lives.

Such is Life!

Printed in Dunstable, United Kingdom